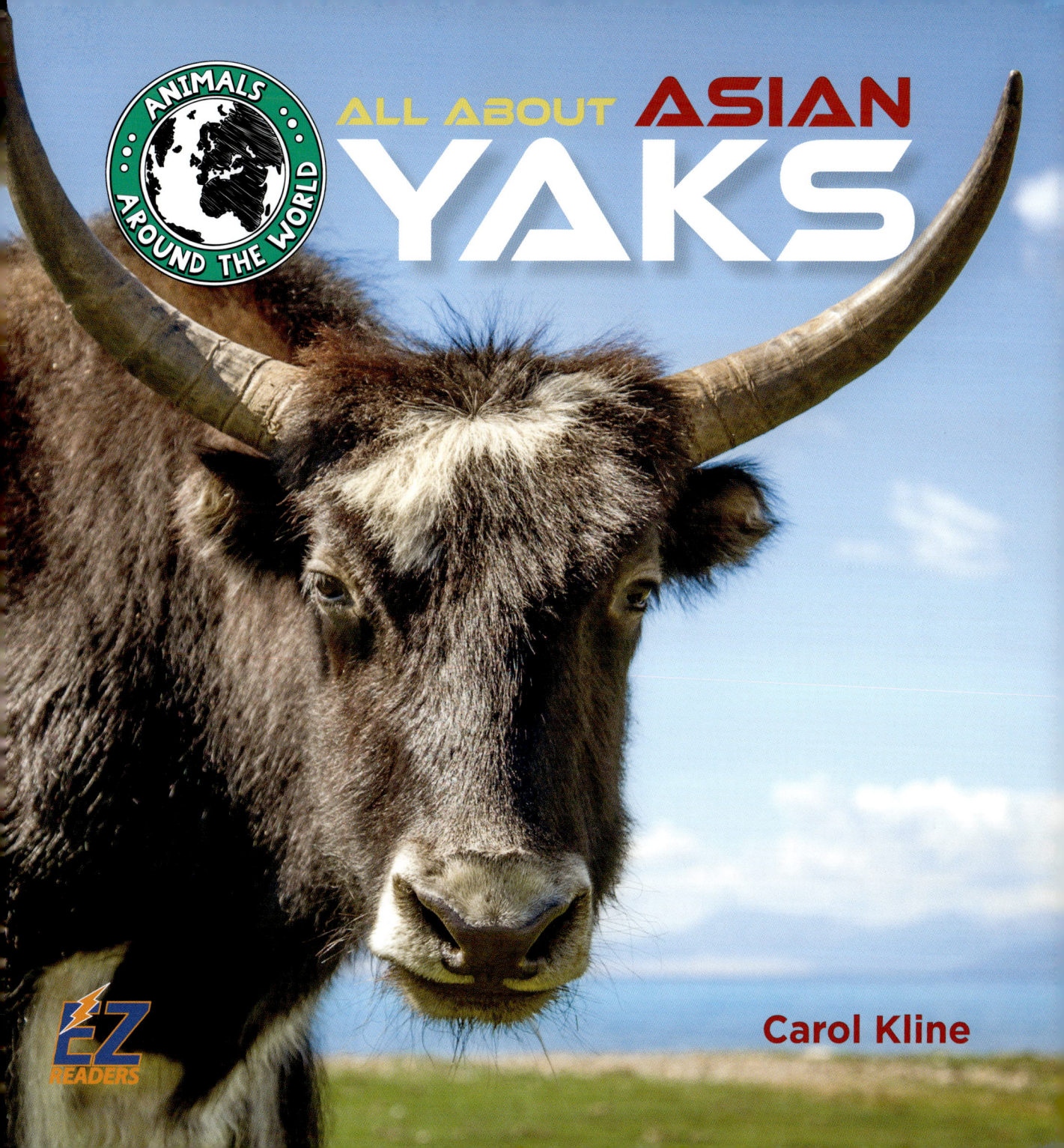

ANIMALS AROUND THE WORLD
EZ READERS

ALL ABOUT ASIAN YAKS

Carol Kline

Creating Young Nonfiction Readers

EZ Readers lets children delve into nonfiction at beginning reading levels. Young readers are introduced to new concepts, facts, ideas, and vocabulary.

Tips for Reading Nonfiction with Beginning Readers

Talk about Nonfiction
Begin by explaining that nonfiction books give us information that is true. The book will be organized around a specific topic or idea, and we may learn new facts through reading.

Look at the Parts
Most nonfiction books have helpful features. Our *EZ Readers* include a Contents page, an index, and color photographs. Share the purpose of these features with your reader.

Contents
Located at the front of a book, the Contents displays a list of the big ideas within the book and where to find them.

Index
An index is an alphabetical list of topics and the page numbers where they are found.

Photos/Charts
A lot of information can be found by "reading" the charts and photos found within nonfiction text. Help your reader learn more about the different ways information can be displayed.

With a little help and guidance about reading nonfiction, you can feel good about introducing a young reader to the world of *EZ Readers* nonfiction books.

Mitchell Lane
PUBLISHERS

2001 SW 31st Avenue
Hallandale, FL 33009
www.mitchelllane.com

First Edition, 2020.

Author: Carol Kline
Designer: Ed Morgan
Editor: Sharon F. Doorasamy

Names/credits:
Title: All About Asian Yaks / by Carol Kline
Description: Hallandale, FL :
Mitchell Lane Publishers, [2020]

Series: Animals Around the World
Library bound ISBN: 9781680204124
eBook ISBN: 9781680204131

EZ readers is an imprint of Mitchell Lane Publishers

Library of Congress Cataloging-in-Publication Data
Names: Kline, Carol, 1957- author.
Title: All about Asian yaks / by Carol Kline.
Description: First edition. | Hallandale, FL : EZ Readers, an imprint of Mitchell Lane Publishers, 2020. | Series: Animals around the world-Asian animals | Includes bibliographical references and index.
Identifiers: LCCN 2018035301| ISBN 9781680204124 (library bound) | ISBN 9781680204131 (ebook)
Subjects: LCSH: Yak—Juvenile literature.
Classification: LCC QL737.U53 K63 2020 | DDC 599.64/22—dc23
LC record available at https://lccn.loc.gov/2018035301

Photo credits: Freepik.com, Shutterstock, mapchart.net

CONTENTS

Yaks look like big shaggy cows. They are related to cows. Some yaks are wild. Others are kept as farm animals.

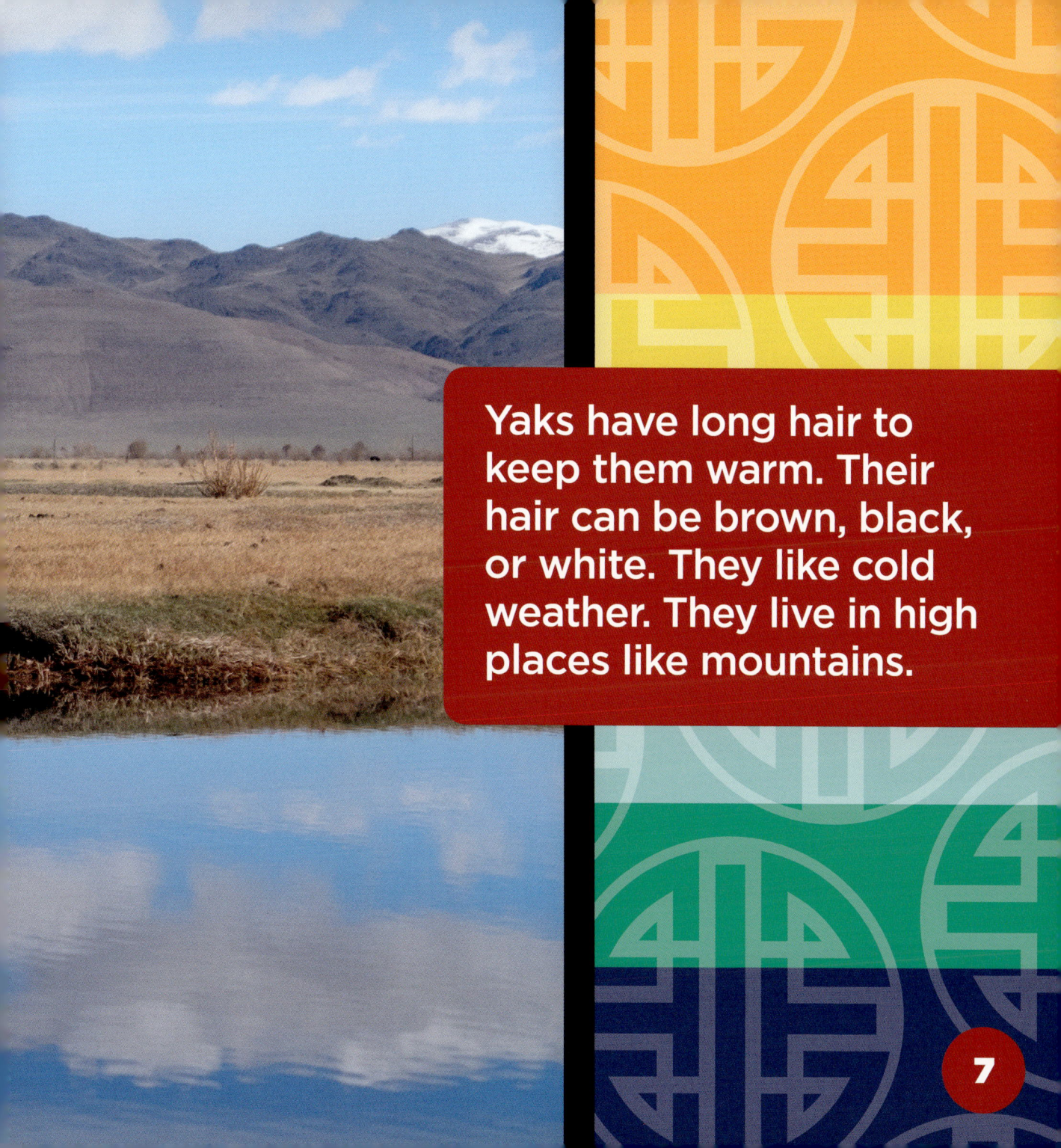

Yaks have long hair to keep them warm. Their hair can be brown, black, or white. They like cold weather. They live in high places like mountains.

A yak's tail is long and bushy. It looks like a horse's tail.

Yaks are heavy animals with short strong legs. Their ears are small. Their forehead is wide.

Yaks have long horns on their head. The horns are longer than your arm.

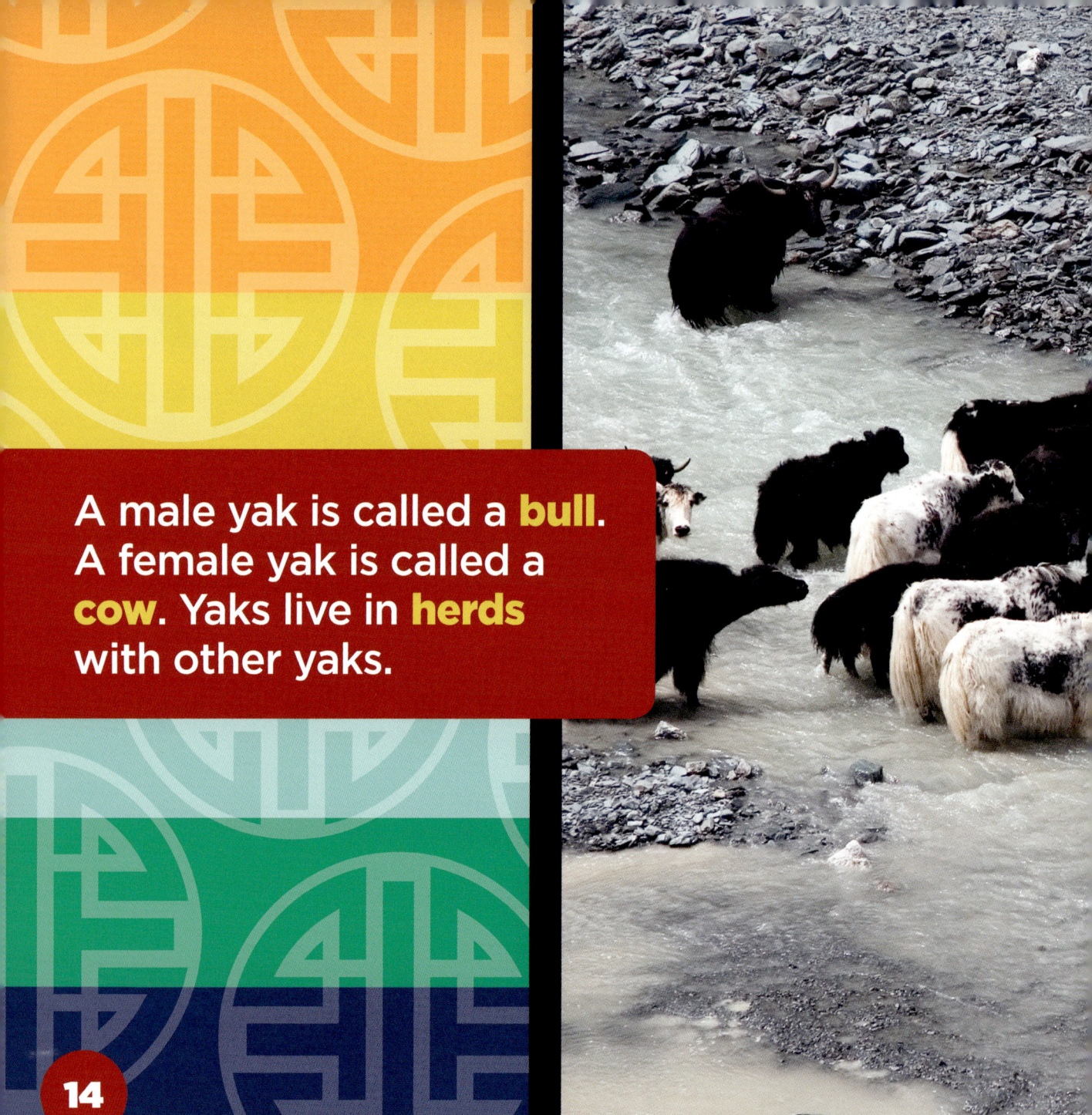

A male yak is called a **bull**. A female yak is called a **cow**. Yaks live in **herds** with other yaks.

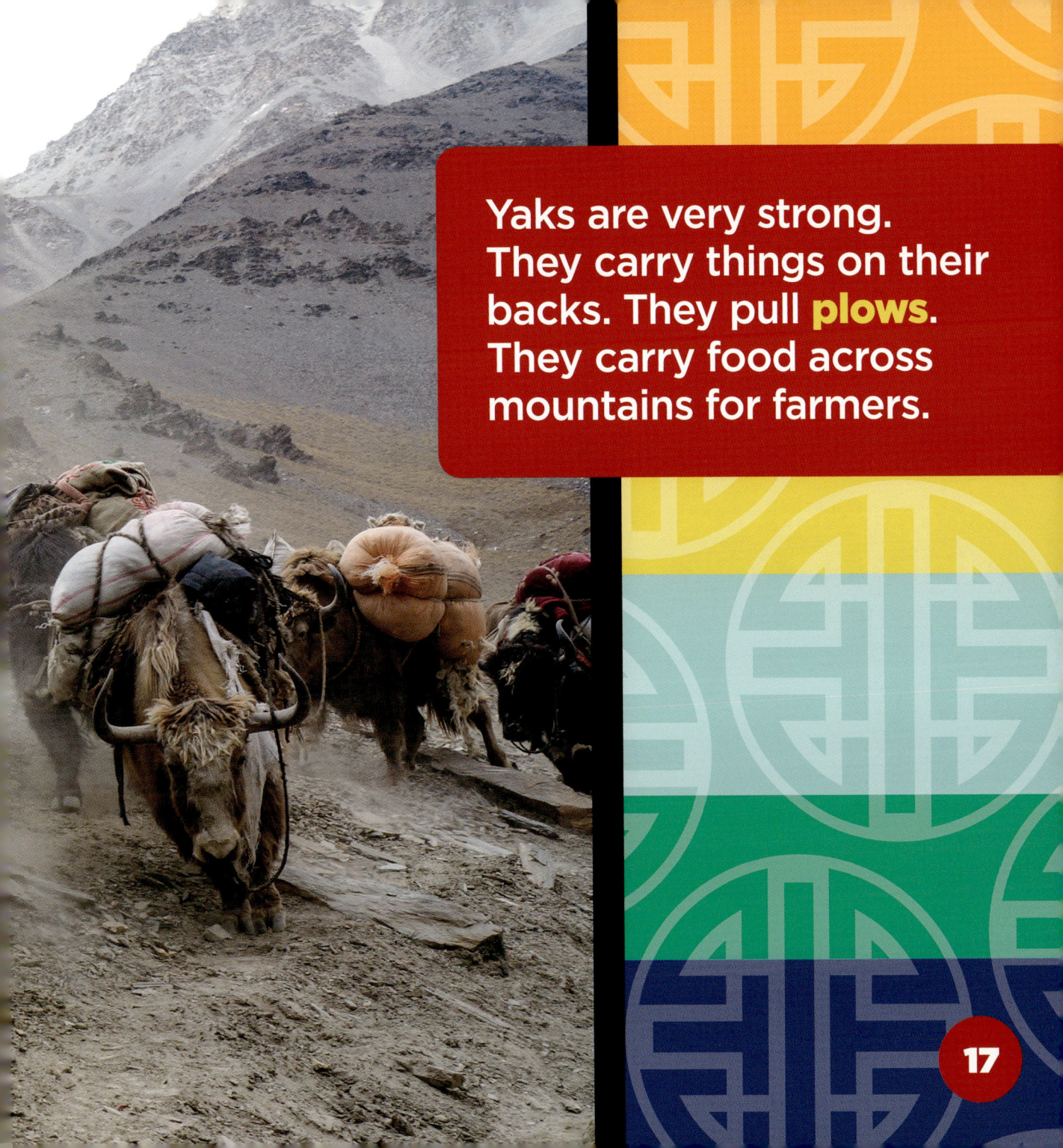

Yaks are very strong. They carry things on their backs. They pull **plows**. They carry food across mountains for farmers.

People use yaks for their meat, milk, and fur.

18

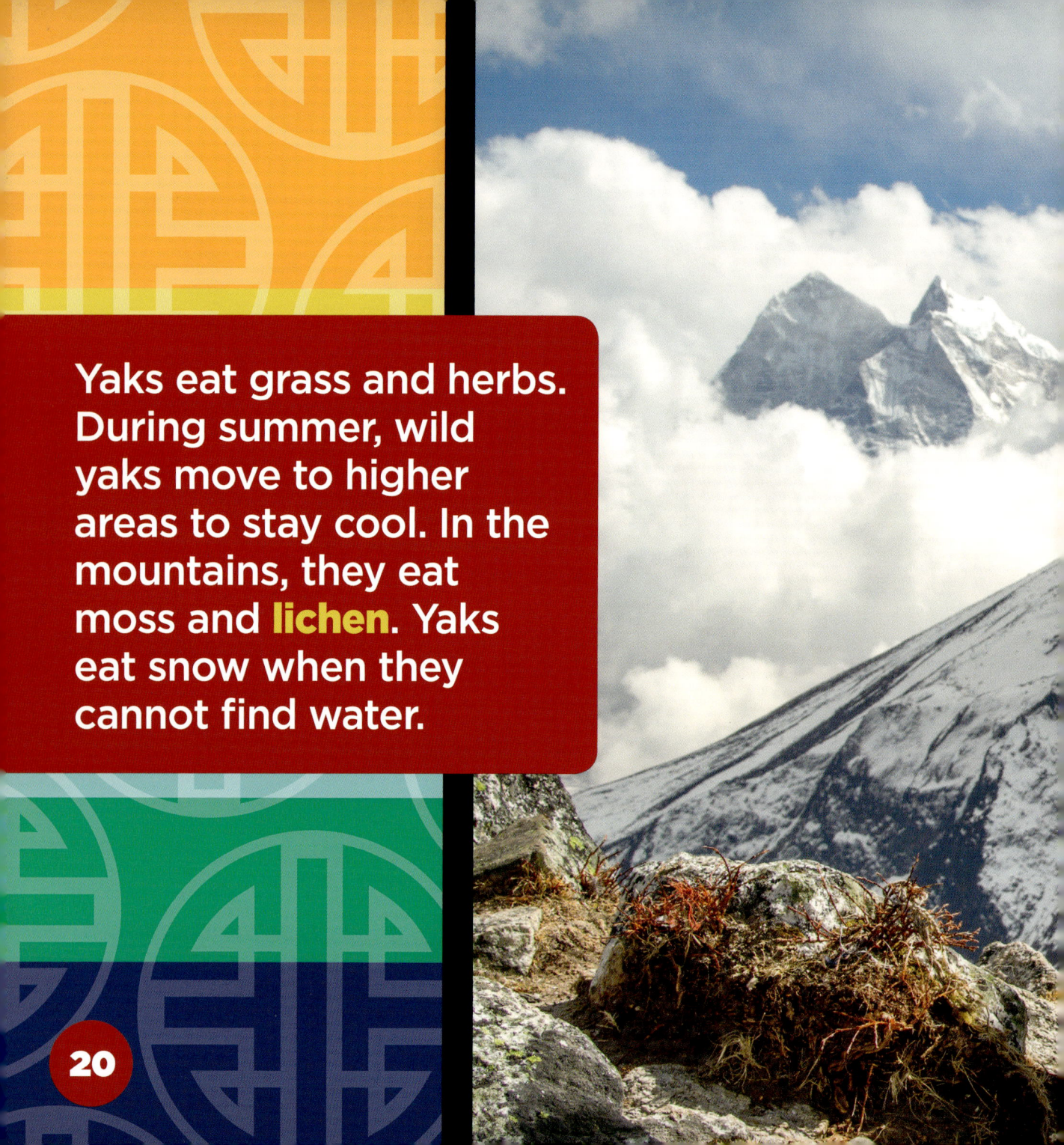

Yaks eat grass and herbs. During summer, wild yaks move to higher areas to stay cool. In the mountains, they eat moss and **lichen**. Yaks eat snow when they cannot find water.

WHERE DO YAKS LIVE?

Most wild yaks (90 percent) live in the Changtang National Nature Reserve in Tibet. Yaks also live in areas of India, China, and Russia.

INTERESTING FACTS

- In China, yaks are called "hairy cattle."

- Females have a **calf** every two years.

- Yaks do not smell bad. Yak hair does not smell bad. Even their poop has little smell.

- Yaks grunt to talk. They do not moo like a cow.

- Yak hair is used to weave ropes, belts, and bags.

- Some yaks live in the United States on farms.

- Wild yaks live about 20 years.

PARTS OF A YAK

Head
Yaks have small ears and a wide forehead. They have small eyes and a broad **snout**.

Horns
Both males and females have horns. On a male yak, the horns stand out from the sides of the head and then curve forward. On a female yak, horns are smaller and point up.

Body
Yaks can grow from 4 to 6.5 feet tall. They have a hump on their back behind their neck and shoulders.

Hair
A yak's hair, or coat, is dense, long, and shaggy.

Tail
A yak's tail is two to three feet long. It is hairy like a horse's tail.

GLOSSARY

bull
A male yak

calf
Baby yak

cow
A female yak

herd
A group of animals that live or are kept together

lichen
A type of small plant without leaves or roots that grows on rocks and walls

plow
A piece of farm equipment that is used to dig into soil to prepare it for planting

snout
The long nose of a yak

FURTHER READING

Clark, Willow. *Yaks (The Animals of Asia)*. New York: PowerKids Press, 2013.

Johnson, Aida. *Yak: Amazing Pictures & Fun Facts on Animals in Nature*. Independently published, 2016.

Ray, Alma. *Yak: A Children Pictures Book About Yak With Fun Yak Facts and Photos For Kids*. CreateSpace Independent Publishing Platform, 2016.

Stefano, Laura. *Yak: Children's Book of Amazing Photos and Fun Facts about Yak*. CreateSpace Independent Publishing Platform, 2017.

ON THE INTERNET

Interesting facts about yaks
http://justfunfacts.com/interesting-facts-about-yaks/

A video about trekking with yaks in Switzerland
https://www.youtube.com/watch?v=dQMPnzmDvM0

INDEX